Nonsense Rhymes From a **Nonagenarian**

Printed and bound in Canada at McNally Robinson Booksellers.
1120 Grant Avenue, Winnipeg, Manitoba R3M 2A6.

Cover and Interior designed by McNally Robinson Self-Publishing
www.mcnallyrobinson.com/selfpublishing

First Edition
978-1-77280-226-9

Nonsense Rhymes From a **Nonagenarian**

My Life in Rhyme

To Allen.

By

Roy White

Acknowledgements

Lisa Taylor for typing, organizing, and working with the publisher.

My granddaughter Erica for encouraging me to write and publish the book.

1.

Do you think the world is fair?
I am ninety and I don't care!
Do you think the world is going to pot?
I own some shares so I hope it's not!

2.

When you're young you look ahead

When you're old you look back instead

You remember all past good times

You get old you resort to rhymes!

3.

When I was a child

Two people outside my home

Treated me as full grown.

They listened to me as an adult.

Pleasure and confidence was the main result.

4.

I was born in '28

Maybe a little too early or maybe too late!

So I lived through all of the 1930's

And I can tell you why they were called the dirty's!

5.

I was fourth in a family of five

Four of whom are still alive.

My grandpa lived for a century plus

His DNA must be installed in us!

6.

I had my birthday and nobody came!

You may think that that's a shame.

But I'm still here by my own self,

And I don't feel that I'm on the shelf!

7.

I have a dog and she likes me.

I like to have her on my knee!

She's such a wonderful companion

And not at all is she demanding!

8.

When you're old you aim to
survive.

No one leaves the world alive!

When you're young your goals are
varied

But the aim to succeed has never
varied!

9.

My brother died in WWII

We lost a part of my mother too!

A disturbing loss of a mother's first!

To have lost him in war was still the
worst!

10.

I attended a one room school
Every day – that was the rule!
After a dust storm I would open the door
And push two inches of dust on the floor!

11.

You should come and dine with me!
Then I think that you would see
What it's like to be really old
And see the validity of what you've been told!

12.

I love to cook, I really do

Today I made some groundnut stew!

You may not know what groundnut is

So I leave you with this simple quiz!

13.

Most voices I can't hear,

So to talk with someone I must get near!

Most find that it's OK,

But some of them push me away!

14.

While on the tractor I love to sing
I knew the words to everything!
But people said I caused them pain!
Now I only sing beside a train!

15.

Do you think being old is any fun?
I can't jump and I can't run.
But fortunately I like my rum
And I know where the rum comes from!

16.

Being old is really not all bad
Many things can make me glad!
Hearing from family is a very good thing
I love to hear the telephone ring!

17.

I realize now that I am alone
Except for my dog and she has her bone!
But I can sleep in as long as I like
Or take my nice dog outdoors for a hike!

18.

Things have really changed since I was a boy!

Some of those changes don't bring me joy.

Ground owls and gophers are very hard to find.

Prairie chickens and badgers are mostly in my mind!

19.

Some changes have improved the world

Cars and farm equipment are much better than old!

Change is the only thing that does not change

But not when I was a kid at home on the range!

20.

I was at the straw stack in '39,
Watching the work of our threshing gang.
That's when Hitler went to war.
All the men decided they'd even the score!

21.

After the harvest they joined up fast!
They had found a job at last!
That's when the women came taking their place!
They worked in the war effort discarding their lace!

22.

If you look here then you can see
I still have got my Christmas tree!
I live here all alone
But this still must be my home!

23.

I have not rhymed about the living!
I find that they are much less forgiving!
I can rhyme about the dead.
They can't complain about what I said!

24.

I like to rhyme when I'm in bed!

I close my mind to things I dread!

I find that crafting a simple verse

Will put me to sleep with no remorse!

25.

Some baby-boomers think I'm cheap,

That my first nickel I did keep.

What they should get through their noodle

Is that I'm not cheap but I might be frugal!

26.

I had a lovely dream last night.
My wife returned all dressed in white.
She settled in her favorite chair
She looked so calm and debonair!

27.

I wonder what to cook today
I'm tired of eating curds and whey!
I'll make a stir fry served with rice
Yes I think that would be very nice!

28.

My little dog doesn't like my dreams,

At least that's what it always seems.

She barks and squirms in agitation

Returns me awake to our man-dog nation!

29.

Old sometimes makes your brain feel stupid!

Gone are the days when you thought of Cupid!

Now I only look for sleep!

And hope when I move my balance I keep!

30.

I like to think about my life
The good, the bad and even some strife!
And when I can put my thoughts to rhyme
Then I can feel I have lived a long time!

31.

I sit by the window very discreet
With both my eyes upon our street.
I see students heading to University
I hope they learn to appreciate diversity!

32.

When I was young I had great
ambition!

But I never seemed to find the right
condition!

So I decided to become a teacher

It paid slightly more than becoming
a preacher!

33.

As I grew old I became interested in
stock.

I used my savings and I lost a lot!

Then I grew lucky and made quite a
lot!

Now I am happily investing in pot!

34.

When I was young I broke my leg

And then I went to Winnipeg!

They strung me up with rope and weights,

It took a long time for me to wear my skates!

35.

I went to Brandon University

Back then there was not much diversity!

Now students come from around the world

At least that is what I've been told!

36.

I have a mice infestation!

That doesn't help my own digestion!

But I have traps throughout the house

And every day I catch a mouse!

37.

My little dog can manipulate me

She likes to climb up upon my knee!

She looks at me and talks with her eyes

And that is really no surprise!

38.

You know I have no complaints
My little dog is really a saint!
She keeps my life going happily
She performs her magic rapidly!

39.

I watched TV all day long
Do you think that could be all wrong?
Without TV I would be all alone
It makes my house feel like a home!

40.

I am amazed how each new generation

Gradually grows up and rules the nation!

Such a generation once included me

Now I have worked myself into antiquity!

41.

I have trouble going to sleep
And I am tired of counting sheep!
But usually at 2:00 am I pass away
And sleep periodically until late the next day!

42.

How does it feel living alone?
Well, I still reside in our shared home!
I feel especially lonely walking up the stairs
We used to do everything working in pairs.

43.

If life is a book then at my age
I'm getting close to the final page!
If I'm in the last chapter
My offspring must work for what is after!

44.

I really love Christmas celebration
As it unfolds across the nation!
I really like all the Xmas lights
I wish they would keep them on all night!

45.

I also like big family dinners
As I grew up they were all winners!
My mother could make divinity fudge
That was the best candy ever judged!

46.

In '29 there was great alarm
The debt adjustment took Dad's farm!
It took him ten long years to pay
By selling livestock and bailing hay.

47.

Nobody knows what the future brings

Nobody has control of things!

Nobody knows what happens when we die

But a loved one knows enough to cry!

48.

I just made my little dog her dinner

I think it really was a winner!

Sometimes I think she overeats

That's because I feed her treats!

49.

I have now written thirty-four
Do you think I have any more?
If I keep working and stay alive
I could reach one hundred by
ninety-five!

50.

I had a wonderful dream last night
Not only that but I slept all through!
The sad part of all that is true
I don't have anyone to tell it to!

51.

Things can be dangerous when you
work on a farm

You had to be careful that you
didn't come to harm!

When you were milking you could
be kicked by a cow

Or have a runaway with horses
hitched to a plow!

52.

In the 40's we had many straw piles

They were in the fields for miles and miles!

Often at night they were set ablaze

I see those as the good old days!

53.

The Bennet buggy was an invented contraption

It was made from a Model T adaption!

More comfortable than the old democrat

And it didn't need gas so that was that!

54.

During the war sugar was on ration

Yet mother canned fruit with a passion!

You were allowed extra sugar to preserve

I think my dad always got more than we deserved!

55.

I grew up eating cracked wheat porridge

Made from wheat we kept in storage!

Topped with farm cream and sugar that was brown

The stuff I buy now I can barely keep down!

56.

I watch Lawrence Welk every Sunday night

I think he plays music just right!

My offspring they just hold their nose

I hope you are not one of those!

57.

To hell with you, to hell with me,

To hell with everyone I see!

I guess you can tell its been a bad day

And that 'to hell' feeling won't go away!

58.

We grew up on a farm near
Underhill

We thought their store was
wonderful!

We could buy one cent candies

We thought they were all just
dandies!

59.

As you probably know by now I am
really a country boy

I loved the country as you can see

But because of my many allergies

The country just didn't love me!

60.

I moved away and became a teacher

I wasn't cut out to be a preacher!

For twenty years I plied my trade

And then another choice I made!

61.

I have good neighbours on my street

They are people I like to meat!

It's nice not to practice neighbour alienation

They are the best across the nation!

62.

Our horses could cause us a surprise

As encephalitis closed their eyes!

They charge through gates and ran through fences

This disease had stolen all their senses!

63.

I just got a picture of Whitewater School

That was where I broke a rule!

I got the strap while in grade one

And now, in retrospect, that was fun!

64.

I phones, I phones everywhere

I ignore them I don't care!

When I was young barbed wire
phones were an innovation

Now the wireless rules the nation!

65.

Today was special because of sun
dogs in the sky

I phoned my friends –they wonder
why?

Until they went outside to see

Then they called up thanking me!

66.

R B Bennet was our Prime Minister

And his '30 legislation was almost sinister!

He gave out bonuses to farmers who sold wheat

People on the prairies had none so got none-wasn't that sweet!

67.

In the 50's our numbers soared

Our military returned – those who escaped the sword!

We called our offspring baby boomers

They insist they weren't just rumors!

68.

Someone suggested I was cheap

I suggested that opinion he could keep!

But please get it through your noodle

A product of the thirties might just be frugal!

69.

If you find you start a fire

Sometimes when you use your dryer

Here is a useful little hint

Please, please remove all the lint!

70.

Being old has got some perks
I never have to show up for works!
Today I didn't arise 'till eleven
I felt so good it could have been heaven!

71.

Please don't ask me why I rhyme
I guess it helps to pass the time!
I live alone with my little dog
And I don't have an internet blog!

72.

I have a book dated 1867

Just like it was sent from Heaven!

It was given to my 13 year old grandfather

It was given for writing with a point shaped feather!

73.

The ‘me too’ movement is a blessing

Women don’t need enforced caressing!

Our Teachers’ Union established equal pay

All employees need that today!

74.

The 30's and the 40's appear often in
my rhymes

Both were very trying and
troubling times!

The 50's brought home soldiers and
freed up money

The following years turned out to
be sunny!

75.

I was a farm kid and when we came to town

The town kids would try and put us down!

I was not good when it was time to fight

But I was really good when it came time for flight!

76.

The world is changing and it doesn't include me

All around things are as different as they can be!

Here I am sitting by myself at home

I have earned the time to be alone!

77.

I grew up in Hartney, a very pretty town

Now I see on TV that Front Street is falling down!

Main Street was unique beside the R.R. track

It makes me sad and I'm not sure I'm going back!

78.

Last year no one died on a U.S.
commercial flight

That news allows airline fliers to
sleep at night!

I would like to ask them just for fun

How many U.S. citizens died from a
gun!

79.

Age has cut my indignation

Now I depend more on regulation!

To lose at the Olympics should be
no shame!

After all their efforts it's just a game!

80.

There is one thing about living alone
It means I am the only one at home!
That I find is really a shame!
There's never any one else to blame!

81.

Since my wife passed I am alone
As time passes I like my home!
I realize that I should keep fit
But mostly I watch T.V. and sit, sit, sit!

82.

I still play tennis
But I'm no longer a menace!
I still hit the ball if the ball I see
But often now the ball will hit me!

83.

I love beans which are good for the heart
But beans also cause vapors to part!
So if you're with me and I start to cough
I suggest that you really should back off!

84.

Twice a week I go shoot pool

I learned to play when I was in school!

I have some friends who join me there

We usually have four so we play as a pair.

85.

Last night we had a big blizzard

Mother Nature is an artistic wizard!

She coated all the trees and bushes and buried all the sand

In the morning I went out to a Winter Wonderland!

86.

I feel like an old, old tree
Stuff is growing all over me!
My dermatologist calls each a wisdom spot
Wisdom? Wisdom it is not!

87.

Why don't some people honour their parents until they are dead?
I guess we're too concerned with life and getting ahead!
If I could meet with my father and mother
I would be pleased to tell them I would chose no other!

88.

My driver stopped at a new space

I opened the door and fell on my face!

The next two weeks I spent in hell

I guess I should improve my behavior
when I get well!

89.

When young you think you will live
for ever

You will take on any endeavour!

When you are old you only wish for
health

Most people would trade it for their
wealth!

90.

Spring is my favorite season on the prairies

All the birds return – ducks, geese, robins and even canaries.

They build their nests and raise their youngsters

Only crows feed out of dumpsters!

91.

Nobody knows for sure what
happens when we die

Religion tells us there is a heaven in
the sky.

I have tried to figure but I just don't
know

I guess I will have to wait and find out
when I go!

92.

My best time as a boy was to get on a horse

Back then we all rode bareback of course!

My last wish would be to mount a lusty steed

And head down doomsday trail at a record speed!

93.

I have a happy little dog

Half Pomeranian half pug so she's a
little bit of both

She talks with her tongue, her tail
but mostly with her eyes

Which make her seem very, very wise!

94.

If we meet a person from another land

I believe we should greet them with an
extended hand

If we could get the whole world under
one huge steeple

I would like to tell them that we are all
just people.

95.

I have now lived with five generations

I have watched each of them build their nations

I have found it interesting to watch each reign

They all have grown taller and uncreased their brain!

96.

My father loved animals – sheep,
horse, cows and goats.

He fed them all with hay and good
oats.

His animals were really worth
seeing

He was a remarkably kind human
being!

97.

We had a wonderful horse her name was Jean

She could run fast and was a real beauty queen!

I rode her bare back and she would always go fast

I left the farm then so she was my last!

98.

What a summer-it was hot and dry

Hardly ever a cloud in the sky!

I was a kid all through the thirty's

I guess that's why I have rain worries!

99.

During the thirty's we all watched the sky

Sometimes there would be a cloud rolling by!

My dad would say just look at their track

They are empties and on their way back!

100.

I can identify Baby Boomers and Millenials on the spot

You might think it difficult but it really is not!

Hand them a Kleenex to wipe their nose

If they discard it, its one of those!